JAMES CHALK, FAIR BUYER OF LIGHTNING

OR; PEACE IS A PILE OF MINT

TIM DEMOSS

Copyright © 2025 by Tim DeMoss

All rights reserved.

No part of this book may be reproduced in any form or by any electronic or mechanical means, including information storage and retrieval systems, without written permission from the author, except for the use of brief quotations in a book review.

This book is a work of fiction. All characters, locations, and occurrences in this book are the product of the author's imagination. Any similarities between persons living or dead are entirely coincidental.

Cover design includes modified versions of the following public domain artworks, provided courtesy of the Metropolitan Museum of Art: 'Landscape' by Ralph Albert Blakelock (1885-95); and the lithographs 'Moonflower', 'Jessamine', and 'Clover' from the *Flowers* series, issued by Goodwin & Company and printed by George S. Harris & Sons for Old Judge Cigarettes (1890).

For Theodora, who looks closely.

FIG **01.** ROUGH MAP OF CLOVER
COUNTRY, SURROUNDING PROMISE

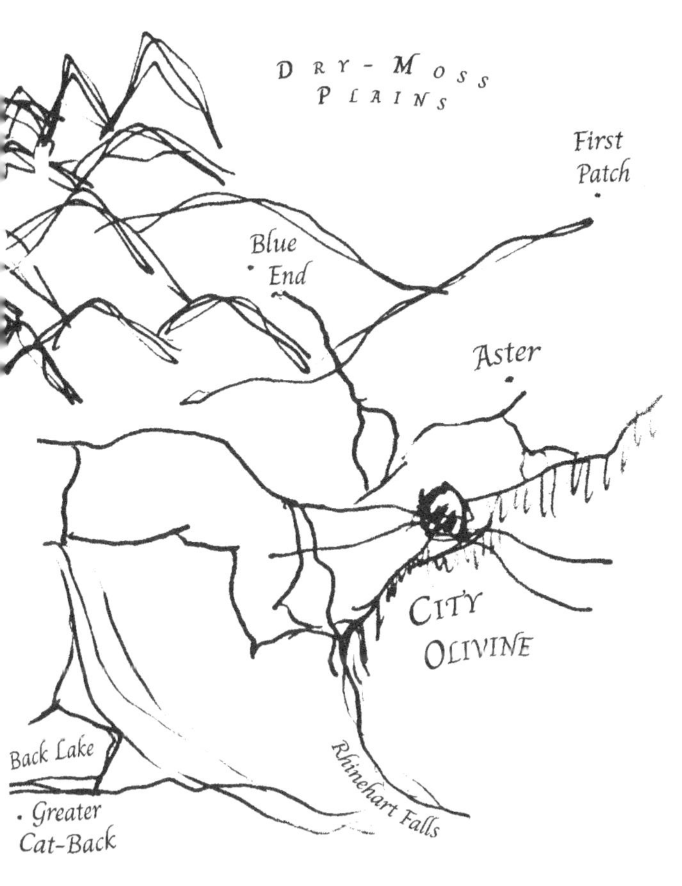

DRY-MOSS PLAINS
First Patch
Blue End
Aster
CITY OLIVINE
Back Lake
Rhinehart Falls
Greater Cat-Back

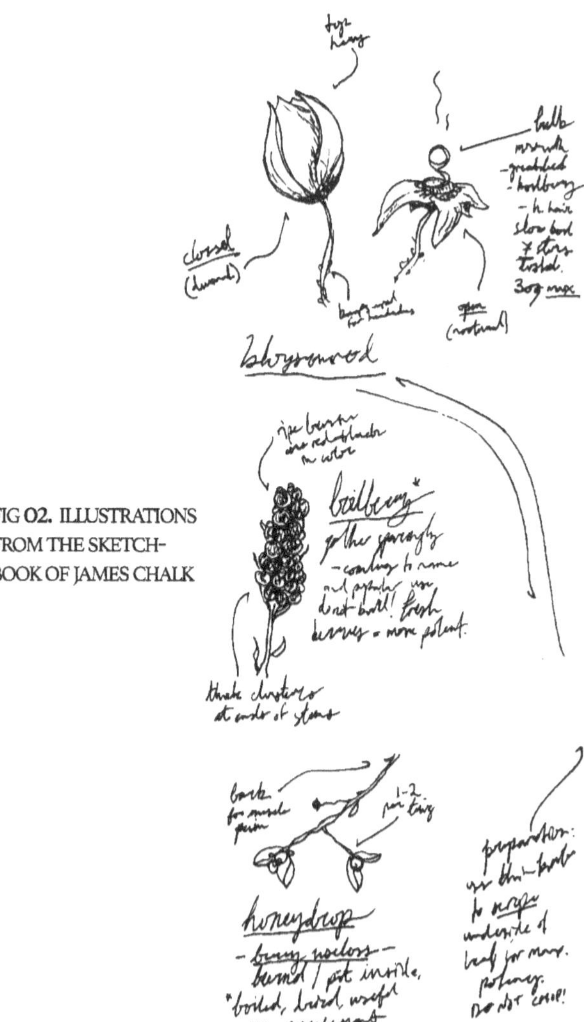

FIG **02.** ILLUSTRATIONS FROM THE SKETCH- BOOK OF JAMES CHALK

blade will have
a slight blue
tint in summer

pine root

- poorly named
- grasses useless,
  miniature tuber
  ~2in. below soil
  removes most warts,
  spots, pustules,
  etc. Mix w/
  bullberry for stinging
  effect. Paste or
  mixture.

crush w/
pestle and
mortar

flowers
effective in
blossom tea

gizzwort

- in small
  doses, tips of
  blossoms mixed
  in hot water assists
  sleep. 3ppc

induces
nausea —
use if poison
long been
suggested

middleclover

- intestinal discomfort
- 4 leaves, irregular
- wiry stem
- common
- pink variety
  attracts bees &
  other pollinators

pollen
for poison
(all ages)

greatleaf

longish, light leaves
w/ irregular internal vein.
— used in finders
  brought — see blizzardwood

leaves not
yet mature;
wait ~6 mos
before harvest

internal
root system
produces offspring
plants irregularly

We are all sculptors and painters, and our material is our own flesh and blood and bones.

— HENRY DAVID THOREAU,
WALDEN

CONTENTS

1

BLOSSOMROD

'A child! A child!' A voice cried out from the road.

James Chalk looked up. He saw the source of the sound through his store window—a frantic, flailing man in black. The man headed straight for him and opened the shop door. He stood, panting, sweating, in the doorway.

James spoke first. 'A child, sir?'

The man was near tears. 'Please,' he said. 'My daughter.'

'Has she fallen ill?' asked James, reaching instinctively for a pile of dried middle-clover.

'No, no!' cried the man. 'Worse, sir. She has vanished.'

James put the clover down. 'Vanished?'

'From her very bed, sir,' said the man.

But for the rustle of dried herbs hanging from the rafters, the shop was silent. Then—

'How can I be of help to you, sir?' asked James, carefully.

'Oh, please,' said the man, earnestly, 'please do not pretend. I know you have skill with mixed medicines.'

'To heal the body, to calm the spirit, yes,' murmured James, 'but to find? To recover what is lost?'

'It is possible,' said the man. 'I know it is.'

'It is forbidden,' said James.

'It is possible,' said the man.

The moon hung a hammock in the sky. James's hair shone whiter than usual in its light. Clover padded his steps. It was not yet morning or anywhere near it, but dew wet his boots nonetheless. In his hand he held a basket. In this basket was— nothing, yet. A few steps more and the meadow gave way to roots and rocks and the thickness of forest. James paused and prayed. He continued on.

Thoughts of risk floated through his mind like dandelion tufts. The area was safe enough, if you knew where to walk. The plants would not harm him either. He had been their friend and companion these thirty years. No, he thought, stepping over a stone. The danger was in the people he was trying to heal.

By moonlight and starlight and a keen sense of the woods he reached his destination in three quarters of an hour's time. A ravine, dark and deep, that cleft the forest in two. The crickets were noisiest here.

Seeing the black ravine at night reminded James that some darknesses were darker than others.

He prayed again. It was then that he pulled out of his pocket a curious thing. It was a little blue bottle, built of glass and one-third full of thick liquid. The liquid was blue like gas and bright like fire, and it swirled slowly and sparkled a little as it did. James held the bottle before him, and, able by its light to see the tips of his feet and the treacheries of the path, stepped slowly down into the ravine.

It was at the bottom that he found it—a small patch of yellow blossomrod. Their petals were open, drinking in the scant moonlight the night afforded. The open petals exposed milky-white pistils, flush and full. James carefully, slowly, plucked three flowers of their pistils and dropped them, glowing, into his basket. The three plants, so harvested of their vitals, shriveled. 'I am sorry,' James whispered.

He knew enough to leave most of the plants

alone. The patch would stay healthy. New flowers would grow back. This patch was a secret most precious, a source of pride as well as plants. He trusted no one but himself with its use or its upkeep.

Three bulbs of blossomrod. He would need other plants as well, but none of them as rare—or as illegal—as this.

A breeze. A chill. The smell of fresh-plucked plants. James yawned and realized he had been standing still for several minutes. He wiped his eyes with the back of his hand and yawned again. By the light of his little blue bottle, he picked his way out of the ravine and headed home.

2

INFUSION

THE DIM LIGHT of near-dawn found James hard at work, eyes reddened again from sleeplessness and the fumes of his burner. A bright yellow liquid bubbled slowly in front of him. Herb and pestle and mortar speckled his workbench. His nose, usually so finely attuned to the slightest difference in odors, was growing blind. The scent of boiling blossomrod was pungent. Not unpleasant, but difficult to miss. It was a dangerous herb to brew here in town.

A rap at the door. A pause. Two more raps, a third.

James called out. 'We are closed.'

'Open,' said a voice.

James stepped to the door and spoke through it. 'What brings you?'

'Three, eleven, fourteen,' whispered the voice. 'For God's sake, open.'

James opened. The man stood outside, cloaked and looking for all the world like someone with something to hide. 'Come in, come in,' said James, pulling the man inside. He closed the door behind them. 'Do you have it?'

The man held out a small folded cloth that must have been white at some point in its life. James took it and examined it. Several dark hairs were stuck to its surface.

'Are you sure these are your daughter's?'

The man nodded fervently. 'The cloth is from her pillow, sir.'

James turned his back to the man and, taking one of the hairs between his fingers, dropped it into the bubbling burner. A puff of smoke. A stir. The potion ran clear, clear as water, thick as honey.

James began to pour the mixture into a vial. The man watched over his shoulder, breathing heavily. 'And you are certain,' he asked, weakly, 'that this will bring me to her?'

James handed him the vial and placed a hand on his shoulder. 'If she is anywhere to be found, it cannot fail.'

The man took James's hand from his shoulder and squeezed it. 'I will repay you a thousand times, sir—'

'Please,' said James. 'No pay.'

The man was appalled. 'But—'

'But—' said James, 'you must tell no one I

have made this for you.' His voice grew serious. 'Drink it here. Leave the vial. Find your daughter. Explain it however you like—an act of God, a lucky chance, your wits—but I gave you no potion. There was never any potion.'

He looked around at his shelves, then back to the man. 'I've grown fond of this shop. I would like to keep it.'

The man shook his hand gratefully. 'Of course, sir, of course, sir—I'd never want trouble to fall on your head, sir. Who'd be curing our headaches, now?'

James released the hand and smiled. 'Thank you.'

They stood in silence. A rooster crowed. The man shifted his weight and laughed nervously. 'Well,' he said, 'better get going, I suppose.' He uncorked the vial and lifted it to his eyes. He tracked its swirling colorlessness uneasily. 'Feels unnatural, this stuff,' he said. 'Not that I'm ungrateful, of course—ah, the *hell* with it!'

He downed the mixture in one gulp. He closed his eyes and breathed and wriggled the joints in his fingers. His nostrils dilated. 'Ah—I feel—oh—*my*—'

He looked up at James and his eyes were changed. James felt the satisfying thrill of work done properly. 'Do you see her?' he asked.

'No—not see—but I hear her, I hear her lute —I feel—I know where to walk—excuse me.'

The man walked to the door, and, with a bow, he was gone.

James walked to his windows and opened the shutters. Daylight was nearly here. The street was empty. The rooster crowed again. Morning, thought James, and he felt the buildup of bleariness in his eyes. Morning and time for sleep.

The shop could wait a few hours today. James closed the shutters and let the dark fall thick and welcome. He breathed, in, out, and without undressing he found his cot and fell asleep.

3

THE FINDING

HE AWOKE to a shout in the street. He scrambled to the door and opened it. Two children stared at his tired face as they ran by. 'The river! To the river!' he heard them say to one another. He watched them disappear.

With a sinking feeling in his stomach he threw on his boots and followed.

The river was not far from James's shop. He ran for only a few minutes before he saw it, rushing, winding, laced with lilies. He slowed and stopped well before he reached the bank.

The two children who had run ahead of him were just joining a crowd of some twenty townsfolk on the riverbank. The crowd stood in a circle, surrounding something James could not see. From within the circle—a scream, a cry. James recognized the voice. He heard sorrow in it—the screamer's. He heard ruin in it—his own.

A woman in the crowd-circle turned. She saw him and *pointed.* 'It's him! The very apothecary!' The circle parted and James saw what he already knew must be at its center. The man had found his daughter. She lay, limp and dark and drowned, across her father's lap. He stroked her hair and added his tears to her river-wet face. And there was a churchman there beside him, giving comfort, who turned to face James with reprobation. And James knew the man had told the town all.

He turned and ran. He ran across a little stone bridge and across the hill on the other side and into and through the forest. Only once he reached unfamiliar ground did he stop to gather his breath. He found himself at the top of a cliff, above the forest he had so recently foraged in.

In the distance, in the town, he saw smoke. A tear of anger dripped onto his cheek. He could imagine the smell—pine boards mixed with a thousand rare herbs, burning all at once, together.

4

THE FARMER

She'd left the candle on. Her eyes snapped open and flitted to the nightstand. The candle sat in its brass holder, cold and dead. Safe. Amity breathed a sigh of relief. Must have been a dream.

The wooden bedframe creaked beneath her shifting weight. She sniffled. Her brain was awake now. It heard the crickets and the wind in the apple trees. It heard the silence of the sleeping pigs and geese and goats. It heard- she leaned towards the window, and the breeze kissed her face—it heard a *rustle*. She was very still. A rustle from the barn.

She never slept well, anyway, and there was no one else to investigate. Shoes on and lantern lit, Amity Parish stepped into the night.

She opened the door and there he was—a man, white-haired and wet with old rain, plucking at a stalk of grass. He sat with his back against the barn wall, his feet nestled in a pile of hay. He had the appearance of someone trying, but failing, to sleep.

He did not even turn his head as Amity entered. The door creaked and then stopped. Somewhere a cow groaned.

At last the man spoke. 'I apologize for waking you, and for intruding on your property. Could you permit me to stay till morning?'

The words were sincere. Their delivery was rehearsed.

Amity stayed by the door. 'Who are you?'

'I am just tired, ma'am, and passing through.'

'Your name?' she asked.

He turned his face into the light of her lantern, and his eyes were white, and she knew who he was. 'James,' he said.

Amity breathed. 'You are him,' she said, not asking. 'You are the apothecary they ran out of Melvale last week.'

'I ran out of Melvale, at least,' said James. He stood up. 'I understand if my being here poses a threat to your livelihood. I will go. You never saw me.' He stepped towards the door.

'Wait,' said Amity.

James tensed. 'I assure you—'

'No,' she said. 'You misunderstand me.' She

paused a moment before finding her voice. 'Have you any skill with pigs?'

They knelt in the trampled grass of the sty. An enormous sow lay sleeping restlessly before them, trembling and twitching in the lantern-light. James traced his finger lightly around a gash in the pig's flesh. It was a hand's breadth in length and ran along her spine. The skin had closed around the wound but had not settled—even in the harsh yellow light, James could see the angry redness of the tissue. His nail brushed a sensitive spot and the pig shifted her weight.

'She ran under a broken rail in the fence,' said Amity. 'I was away; my neighbor was tending the stock. He cleaned it best he could, which—' she indicated the wound— 'you can see was not enough. When I returned yesterday it was beyond my knowledge to heal.'

She looked at James. 'But now you have come. Perhaps—'

James nodded. 'The things I need can be gathered. But not before morning.'

'I have a room where you can stay.'

James smiled. 'And what will the church in your town say when they find you harboring a magician?'

Amity stood and gathered her skirts. 'The church will not know. Who is there to tell them?'

'You could,' said James, standing alongside her, suddenly tall. 'When the pig is healed.'

Amity did not move. 'I'm not in the habit of sacrificing innocent men.'

James looked surprised. 'You don't believe I made the finder's draught?'

'On the contrary, I'm sure you did,' said Amity. 'But I am hardly convinced that mixing flowers and oils to help a poor man find his daughter is or should be a crime. One would think you'd *killed* her, not *found* her, the way these people talk.'

She spat in the dirt. 'You are lucky. This home is the home of one sympathetic to your cause.'

'I assure you,' said James, 'I have no cause; I am no preacher. I wish only to go back to a shop, someday, somewhere.'

'Perhaps someday you will. But let's start with your room, first,' said Amity. 'You travel quickly. You've come a ways from Melvale.'

'Where am I, then?'

'Promise,' said Amity. 'Or the edge of it. Are you familiar?'

'The name, only,' James said.

Amity held the lantern up to his face. He was tall. His hair *was* white, but his face was young. As young as hers, at least. She locked eyes with him, and his eyes were the strangest of all. From a distance they had been white. Up close they were ghost-gray, barely blue. She saw wonder in them, wonder and power. They did not shrink from the lantern.

She pulled the light away and blinked. 'Are you pursued?'

'I was,' James said. 'No longer.'

'Come, then,' she said.

And they walked toward the house in the silence of night.

5

IN THE SPARE ROOM

THE SOW HEALED RIGHT QUICKLY, but still James remained in the house of Amity Parish. The room was comfortable, the company pleasant; both, at least, superior to what he had endured the week prior in the wet of the woods.

In exchange for his housing and board and safekeeping, James turned his knowledge of herbs to enriching the home and farm of his host. Nights saw him crawling through the forests, foraging, little blue bottle-light guiding his way; days saw him hunched over makeshift burners, stirring, distilling, pouring. He would hand his results to Amity with a few whispered words of instruction— 'for the apple-tree-blight, a few drops on the trunk,' 'this will help you rest, nights,' 'to brighten your kettle.' At first these mixes came unprompted, but, as Amity slowly grew wide-eyed in realization of the skill of the man she now harbored in her guest room, she began to request some herself.

Her requests were few and simple. She would leave a bowl of soup and thick slice of bread by his door, then mention in passing she had a slight headache. A vial would find its way to her hands sooner rather than later. She would mention she was tired, drained—there was a mixture for that. All perfectly normal items within the realm of any village healer. James sometimes wondered why she did not simply go to town to buy them.

In these simple requests James felt her toeing around the edge of far greater ones—wanting, but afraid, to ask for things beyond what the church and her own upbringing would allow. The question floated in her mind for days. James could see it hanging, coming loose, nearly falling. He waited for it to fall patiently.

One day it did. Amity lingered a moment after handing him his tray.

He waited. He smelled the soup.

Finally she spoke. 'Say I wanted a cure for a migraine,' she said. 'Lemon balm and lavender. They can sell that in any shop the village.'

'They can, and they do,' he said.

'Say I wanted a child raised from the dead,' she said. 'That is forbidden.'

James put down the tray of soup and folded his arms. 'Forbidden, certainly. Though I'm not sure something so impossible even needs to be illegal. I am sorry—'

Amity waved him off. 'I have no such child. It was just a question. A drink to cause sleep?'

'Guisewort. They can sell that.'

'A way to restore hair?'

'Hound's clover, cow's bone. Also, illegal.'

Amity stood quietly for a few moments. 'Where is the line?'

'Excuse me?'

'Where,' she repeated, 'is the line?'

'Which one?' asked James.

'The line between medicine and magic,' Amity said. 'Between what you practiced in Melvale and what became your exile. What will they let you do? What will they punish you for?'

'You know church doctrine better than I,' said James.

'I know what they tell us,' said Amity. 'I want to know what you think.'

'What I think they believe?' asked James. 'Or what I think they should believe?'

'Either. Both.' Amity was resolute.

James picked up his tray again. He motioned with his head that she should enter the room. 'Please,' he said. 'Come in.'

He sat down. She did the same.

He sighed. 'Where is the line, Amity? As far as what the church thinks—the truth is I doubt even they know. Curing headaches used to be on the wrong side of that line. Now you can buy lemon balm and lavender in the church itself.'

'Lemon balm grows on the river-bank,' said Amity. 'How could it ever have been considered a crime?'

'They've decided it isn't, any longer,' said James, 'though whether that's because they truly believe or because their children had headaches, I cannot say.'

He took a bite of his bread. 'The general statement of the church is this—when a mixture enhances a natural human ability, it is acceptable. All headaches go away on their own, eventually, so they don't mind lemon balm. But when a mixture introduces a new ability, one that was not there before—the finder's draught—it is extra-natural. An abomination.'

'But people *can* find other people, naturally, eventually. Why is the finder's draught illegal?'

James sipped his soup. 'Ask them. Their list is not consistent. Something in my work smacks of heresy, they say. They say they can feel it, when something is magic.'

'*Is* it magic?' asked Amity.

'Does it matter?' asked James, and took another bite of bread. 'They hate the feeling of things they cannot comprehend. People grow wakeful and sleepy in cycles, naturally, so guise-wort and honeydrop are not offensive to them.

But drowned girls do not find themselves, and paintings do not move, and—'

'You can make paintings move?' asked Amity.

'I have heard of it,' said James. 'And truly, I see no reason my abilities should have limits, if my arts were not considered crimes against the church.'

'Why should a moving painting be a crime?' asked Amity. 'I should like to see one.'

James put his cup down. 'The church won't admit it, Amity, but the real test of whether they consider something acceptable or forbidden is whether it makes them feel uncomfortable or not. Whether it threatens their livelihood or their arts. And conversely—' his voice dripped with disdain now— 'if it can make their lives better, they *will* find a way to whitewash and legalize it. Eventually. *That* is what they really think about these things.'

Amity thought for a little. 'And you,' she said, quietly. 'What do you think?'

'I think in a hundred years, they'll make me a saint.' James smiled. 'But they may burn me first.'

6

TIME PASSES

James's residency at the Parish place became an open secret—at least, among those few of Amity's friends in Promise who were more interested in improving their crops and healing their children than in surrendering James. They did not ask questions. They came on pretense of buying or selling or a social call; they left with vials of energy and sleep and growth and power. Artisans came for inspiration. Aged farmers came for strength in their bones. Lovers came to speed along or remedy their courtships. All discreet, and—to James's surprise—most, if not all, bearing the flower of goodwill. In very few of his dealings did he sense any disdain or disgust. Most were purely thankful. Many were actually in awe, staring at the little glass vials as they left, shocked that such a humble place could provide such power.

For his part, James enjoyed the work and his life at the Parish place. Amity insisted he keep the money he brought in from his trade (it would be suspicious, she said, if she were to suddenly prosper without reason). He had hopes that soon he would have enough to leave Promise and travel discreetly to a far country. He would change his hair and begin a new shop among a new populace, one that, if not more accepting, would at least be ignorant of the charges against him.

Amity sat at a small table by the fire, pen and ink and scribble before her. James sat in the corner. He held a lute and played it slowly as he stared at the flames. From time to time Amity added a line of words to the paper.

'What are you writing?' asked James.

'Poetry,' sighed Amity, and scratched out a line several times.

'May I read it?' asked James.

'No,' said Amity, and crossed out another line. 'The going is painful. Someday.'

She crumpled the paper and composed herself with a deep breath. James looked at her understandingly.

She watched him play the lute for a few moments. 'Thank you for playing tonight. How long have you studied?'

'Not long,' he said, plucking.

'You play very well!' she said. 'That lute has hung here for years, but it's never taken to me.'

'The mixtures help,' he admitted with a smile.

'There are mixtures for music?' asked Amity.

'There are, for everything,' said James. He looked at her crumpled poem.

'Is it forbidden?' asked Amity.

James frowned. 'Does that matter to you?'

'No,' she said. 'I only seek to understand.'

'It is forbidden, then,' he said. 'The church hates it. I am surprised you need ask. It goes against core doctrine.'

'But had you not told me, I would assume the skill was natural,' laughed Amity.

'Natural is an empty word,' said James.

He played all through the evening, but spoke no more. Soon Amity took a long drink of guise-wort James had prepared for her and went to bed. Still James played into the night.

At last, the fire bleeding down and the moon dark, he put down his lute and picked up his boots.

7

NIGHT MEETING

THE NIGHT WAS CRICKET-QUIET. The hills around the Parish place stood still and tall and round. Their dirt lay packed beneath the grass, the bushes, the shrub. Above them all walked James. He hummed a slow hum. His basket was full, now, swelled with the good things of the earth. There was nothing more to look for, nothing more to harvest, but the sun was still far off and James was not in a hurry. He plucked idly at a few of the boilberries that drooped over the edge of the basket. He put one in his mouth. His lips tingled pleasantly. He walked on.

His feet took him towards town, but still slowly, still meandering. His eyes looked down, now at his swinging basket, now at his swinging feet, now at the rushing grass beneath. All were washed in the clean blue light of the bottle around his neck. There was only a sliver of moon.

As he walked he thought. He thought of the room he had lost in the fire. He thought of the room he had now at Amity's. He thought of the things he knew and the things he did not, and the third things besides, those he did not know he did not know. He thought of the girl who had drowned in the river. He thought of the father who had found her. He thought of the ache in his feet and the flame in his lungs as he had fled from the angry crowd by the river. As if summoned, the ache and flame returned, and James suddenly felt the need to sit. He did and let his breath calm itself.

The silence fell upon him gradually. He became aware of the coolness of the mossed rock on which he sat. His fingers ran over its surface. Silently he sat. The woods were silent with him.

And then they were not. A rustle—a parting of brush—a boy emerged on the path. Seeing James, he swore and jumped. He did not run. He held a small bag.

'I am sorry to startle you,' said James. He lifted his bottle up to cast some light on the visitor. Even in the blueness, he could see the boy's eyes were shot red from crying.

'What are you doing out here?' asked the boy.

James lifted his basket. 'Plants.' He knew enough to not ask the boy the same question.

The boy stared at him. 'I know you,' he said.

'You're the apothecary hiding out at Ms. Parish's.'

'And I know you,' said James. 'You're the baker's son. Daniel, is it? I sent your mother home with a skin cleanser last week.'

The boy rubbed his face. 'Worked a right charm, it did,' he said, admiringly. He eyed the basket of herbs. 'What do you have there?'

James patted the rock beside him. 'Come and see.'

Daniel sat next to James, the basket between them. 'Point to anything you like,' said James, 'and I'll do my best to explain.'

'These.' Daniel pointed to the boilberries.

James popped one in his mouth. 'They sting your mouth.'

'And what mixture do they make?'

'Truthfully, they just add spice. People like their medicine to taste potent.' He popped another. 'And at this point, I just like the flavor.'

Daniel laughed. 'All right, this one.' He pointed to the guisewort.

'This will put you right to sleep,' said James. 'And this,' he said, pulling at a clump of honeydrop, 'will wake you right up.'

'I know that one,' said Daniel. 'My mother takes it. She still looks tired though.'

'I'm not surprised, with you running around,' said James.

Daniel ignored him. 'So all these need to be picked at night?'

James chuckled. 'Some do for potency. And some you really can only find in the night. This blossomrod, for example—' he tapped a few— 'won't open during the day. But most could be gathered just as well in the daytime. Better, even, or at least faster, with less stumbling about.'

'Then why do you come out at night?'

'At the moment,' James said mildly, 'I'm in hiding.'

The boy looked embarrassed. 'Of course.'

'But I always, always preferred the dark,' said James. 'I've been foraging by moonlight or lamplight as long as I can remember. Maybe it's the cool, or the solitude, or the quiet.'

They sat on the rock that way, man and boy and basket, for some time.

Finally Daniel spoke. 'I think it's stupid.'

'What?' asked James.

'The laws of the church. You, in hiding. Me, stuck with pimpled skin. All of it.'

'You're not stuck anymore.'

'And I thank you, but under their laws I would be. And *you're* still stuck—out here, in the night, wandering!'

'I told you, I like the night. I can stay here quite awhile.'

'But you shouldn't have to.' Daniel was deadly serious now. 'Who are they to say what is and is not forbidden? How dangerous can a plant be?' He gestured to James's basket.

'There are other magics,' said James.

Daniel waited for him to continue, but he did not. A prompt, then, hushed but bold: 'Are there, then, spirits? In these woods? I have heard of them.' His voice was tinged with fear.

James stood and shook his head. 'I mean only that the church is trying its best. That there are forbidden and dangerous things, and lawful and good things—on that the church and I agree. We only disagree on the line that divides them.' He put a hand on Daniel's shoulder. 'But be sure of this—there is a line. And I say be careful of things you do not understand.'

'Do you understand?' asked Daniel.

'Understand what?' asked James.

'I don't know,' said Daniel. 'Good night, then.'

'You don't have to go—'

'No, I better be going. They don't like when I'm gone so long. Good night.' Daniel started down the path.

A few paces on he stopped. 'Can I ask you a question?'

'Go ahead.'

'Will you answer?'

'If I can.'

Daniel pointed to the little blue bottle around James's neck. 'What's in the bottle?'

James did not look down. 'Maybe it's just a lamp.'

'It isn't,' said the boy.

'No, it's not,' said James. 'Good night.'

Daniel smiled and walked off into the dark. James waited until his footsteps faded; then, tucking the bottle into his cloak, he walked the rest of the way home in the dark.

8

GUISEWORT

A MONTH of gathering and living and sleeping passed. All the while James slowly fitted his room with better equipment and wider stock. It was still nowhere near the layout he'd had in Melvale —he sighed often when he thought of the tools and plants he'd left behind—but it was more than serviceable. His days, though full of brews for Amity and his other clients, had still more than enough hours in them to afford him plenty of time for his own alchemical experimentations and studies. He mixed new things. He drank them himself. Sometimes he found what he was looking for; sometimes he found something truly unexpected and wonderful; sometimes he found himself rocking on the floor and vomiting blue clumps of flower petals. Still he continued.

It was during one of these vomiting sessions that the door to his room burst open. Amity appeared. From the light streaming in over her shoulders and around her body, James could tell it was already the afternoon. He'd passed a long night.

Amity looked at his wracked body and covered her face. 'Oh—I'm sorry—I didn't know,' she said. But she did not leave.

James lay on his back, panting. 'Yes?'

'I apologize—it is urgent—' Amity nearly wept. 'Martha's son has run away.'

James rolled over and vomited. 'The baker? Her oldest?'

'Yes. Daniel. She said he left the house last night—a fight, you know—the father's an *awful* —well, he's gone now, he's run off.'

James sat up, painfully. He wiped his mouth. His nose and cheeks were raw and red.

Amity eyed him tearily. 'Daniel may be in serious trouble.'

Her eyes flitted from James to his workbench, then back. She held out a cloth. A few brown hairs stuck to it. 'Could you—'

'It is not hard,' said James, steadily. 'But you understand you are asking me to repeat my crime.'

'Crime!' cried Amity. 'Finding a runaway child—'

'It will reveal me,' said James.

'Martha will not tell.'

'It matters little what she says or does not

say,' said James, staggering to his feet. 'No apothecary in a hundred miles would be fool enough to make a finder's draught now. The church will know. They will beat it out of her. And they will find me here.'

Amity stood still, a solution lying unspoken on her lips. James saw it there and pulled it into the room. 'You will have your mixture,' he said. 'Tomorrow morning. I need more blossomrod.'

He turned away and began to pack his few belongings. He said nothing else.

Amity wavered. She did not know how to tell him that his boots by the spare-room door and his breathing in the night gave her peace. She did not know how to tell him that she believed he would do no harm, had done no harm, had been nothing but blessing and fruit for her and for the village as long as he had lived under her roof.

She didn't know, and she didn't say. Instead, she closed the door.

In the morning his boots were gone and his breathing was elsewhere. The room was empty. The only signs of his existence were the guisewort he'd dried for her, hanging over her door, and a small vial of clear, viscous fluid sitting on her table. There was no note. She took the vial and stepped into the doorway of her home. A morning breeze chilled a single tear that had formed in the corner of her eye.

She shivered and looked at the hanging bundle of dried guisewort. She took a leaf and crumbled it between her thumb and finger; then, scattering the bits to the wind, she strode, vial in hand, to Martha's.

9

CAPTURE

THEY CAUGHT him on the fourth day. He had made a good run of it. But his little blue bottle-light caught the attention of a band of forest watchmen late one night. Now he walked in procession with them, hands behind him, cheeks and knuckles bloody, down the forest path into Promise. James looked at the path beneath his sore feet with fascination. How little he had traveled on this strip of cleared land! How much less had he done so in daytime! The path was as foreign to him as the thickets with their thorns and remedies were to the watchmen who now delivered him to justice.

His lips were dry and cracked.

'A drink,' he asked.

'Conjure one,' said the guard ahead of him, without turning her head.

They passed the Parish place at some distance on their way into town. It was still another twenty minutes' hard march to the center of town, and James was frothing at the lips well before they arrived. They threw him down on his knees before the church. 'Look up,' commanded one.

James did. He saw the church's marble steps; he saw its pillars, carved by hand with ornate imagery of women and men, swimming in lakes, dancing on mountains, singing in fields; he saw its green flags, fluttering from posts, a large unbroken circle of gold in the center of each. Think of the church what he may, James conceded their arts were imaginative and their buildings carried great beauty.

A woman in the green robes of the clergy appeared from within the church. She had black hair that flowed down her back, and in her left hand she held a gold-capped walking stick. James recalled such a stick having some function in the liturgy. Her arms and her neck were covered in green tattoos, and so powerful was her build and so vivid her tattoos that she did not seem out of place among the carved pillars of the church.

She waved a hand and the guards dispersed. A small crowd of villagers had gathered, and they, too, left, until James and the tattooed priest were left alone in the morning mist.

James looked at her eyes. They were green and not unfriendly. They met his own for only a moment, then turned to examine the morning. Her search made James aware of the birds calling. At length she returned her eyes to him.

'Can you walk?' she asked.

'These ten miles,' he said, and stood.

She turned. 'Follow me, please.' She disappeared into the chuch. James spat on the cobblestone—out of necessity, his mouth was flecked with foam—and, mounting the marble stairway, followed.

10

THE BELLY OF THE CHURCH HUMAN

SHE TOOK HIM THROUGH A HALLWAY. The inside was like the out—lavishly designed and decorated, extravagant, orderly, intricate, tasteful. Alcoves lined the wall at intervals. Each held a statue of a sainted figure in the Church's history. James knew many of these statues had been carved by the saints themselves—the original statues, at least—in their final years of life. The copies he saw before him, he knew, had been made by sculptors in the service of the local church. They would travel to see the original, painstakingly chisel a near-identical copy into existence, and return with their treasure.

James had not attended services for many years, but the lore was culturally pervasive, and he knew the figures he passed. They passed St. Paul the Green, who, a thousand years before, had discovered, while painting the hills of his mountain retreat, a new method of producing a particularly lustrous shade of the color green; this was the aptly-named Paulian Green, the church's sacred pigment. His statue was carved from olivine, and his alcove was painted in his namesake. James nodded in respect.

They passed St. Aster of Copple, her quartz figure bearing blue-painted tears. This image James knew well. St. Aster was the mother of the apothic tradition; her *Encylopede Herbales,* though out of date, was in the library of every apothecary, town healer, and home medicine enthusiast. James's lips tightened as he remembered how Aster had died; bound, burning, screaming, tied to a wooden stake among bushels of lemon balm and lavender.

This was, of course, before the Church legalized those herbs and made Aster the patron saint of medicine.

They turned right at the end of the hallway, beneath an archway of carved wheat and fruit and sunbeams, into a windowless stairwell lined periodically with candles. James considered fleeing. They went down, ten steps, twenty, a turn, ten steps more, ten more, a turn—a door, heavy. Through it, a room, large, spacious, almost cavernous, lit by a single shaft of light coming from a hole in the center of the ceiling. James's eyes had grown used to the dark; he was forced to squint and look away from the beam. As his eyes adjusted he saw the room he was in was a sort of lobby or foyer, lined with several doors that led—elsewhere.

A serious man with a shaved head sat at a mahogany desk near the door, reading from a heavily illustrated manuscript. He looked up and brightened. 'A room, Mother?'

'Yes, Elder,' she said. 'The Rhinehart, if it is available.'

The man opened a drawer and fumbled with a set of keys. He walked across the room, shoes clacking, robes swishing, passed through the beam of light for a moment, glowing like an angel, then disappeared into darkness. James could not see him through the light, but he heard the opening of a door. The elder reemerged through the beam of light, bowed to the priest, and returned to his seat.

The priest motioned to James. 'After you.' He shielded his eyes and walked into the beam of light. He paused in the middle and felt the heat on his shoulders.

'By all means, look,' said the priest.

James looked up. Above, through a carved channel of rock and earth several stories tall, he saw—the sun. It was noon.

Temporarily blinded, he let the laughing priest guide him into the Rhinehart room.

She sat him down in a chair and lit a candle. Slowly the vision returned to his eyes. The table was like the elder's desk in the foyer—mahogany, thick, dark. The seats were cushioned. Several dim lanterns hung from the ceiling. The priest sat across from him, her bright eyes staring out of her tattooed face. Above her head, on the back wall, was another statue of St. Aster. The priest noticed James's eyes traveling upward and smiled. 'You are familiar with St. Aster,' she said.

'I owe her a great debt,' James said.

'Then pay it,' said the priest. 'Now, here, with your cooperation.'

James slowly lifted his hands. 'I am unsure of what you mean.'

'You know why you are here.'

'If I have committed a crime—'

'You have,' she said, wearily. 'You twice concocted and distributed a blend of blossomrod bulb, greatleaf, boilberry, and human hair—a finder's draught—with intent and full disregard of Church doctrine regarding the use of extra-natural mixtures, medicines, or substances. Do you deny it?'

'Does it matter if I do?' asked James.

The priest tapped her fingers against the table. 'Not at all. We have sworn statements from three witnesses who spoke with you directly.'

James straightened himself in his chair. 'Then why am I here?'

'Here, and not burning at the stake, as your St. Aster did?' asked the priest.

'Yes,' said James.

'I have not ruled that out, yet,' said the priest, calmly. 'But we are not so reactionary as our predecessors were. St. Aster's execution was a colossal blemish and stain on our history. One we have striven to atone for. I would not make the same mistake.'

'You think I may have the makings of a saint, then,' said James.

The priest laughed. 'Hardly. But you may not need to die.'

She leaned forward. 'You have skill, Chalk,' and James was surprised by the earnestness in her voice. 'Journals of yours were rescued from the fire. I had them requisitioned from Melvale when I heard rumors that you were among us. They are marvelous. Your notes, your illustrations—the connections you make—you are no common healer. And you are certainly no common criminal. Your mind is admirable. And so—' here she trembled in voice— 'I must ask— why?'

James was silent for a moment. 'Why?'

'Why do you, you who possess such natural talent, seek to commune with the extra-natural?'

'Is it not natural to seek growth?'

'Growth!' said the priest. 'The church seeks growth. You seek explosion.'

'I know I am an abomination to you,' said James. 'Charge me and be done.'

'You are not the abomination, Chalk,' said the priest. 'I would save you. I would have you turn yourself to our arts.'

'And to earn this?' asked James.

'You are familiar with our creed?'

'Remind me.'

The priest rang a bell that must have been hanging beneath the table. After a moment, the elder with the shaved head opened the door. 'May I be of service, Mother?'

'A copy of the liturgy, please,' said the priest. The elder disappeared and returned a moment later with a thin book. He handed it to the priest, bowed, and left.

The priest opened the book. 'It is a simple creed,' she said, 'but beautiful.' She offered it to James. 'Will you read it for me?'

'I would prefer to have it read,' he said.

The priest retracted the book. 'Very well.' She began to read.

The Creed of the Church Human

*I believe a god or gods created this
world we live in, river and
mountain, mind and matter;*

*that, their work completed, they
withdrew, to continue in their
acts of creation across time
and space;*

*that our true act of living and
worship now is to create, to use
the minds and the materials
we have received;*

*to carve, dance, paint, heal, and
build;*

*to learn, from others and bitter
experience;*

*that in this way, we might be more
fully human and thus fully
real.*

*I believe in the effort and the
struggle;*

*I believe in the process and the ex-
periment;*

*I renounce the short-cut, the occult,
the extra-natural, and the life
unexamined.*

As I was created, now I create.

She closed the book. 'This is the core. Our laws stem from it. But I assume you are familiar with our laws,' she smiled, 'having broken so many.'

'I am familiar,' he said.

They sat in silence.

'It is a beautiful creed, is it not?' asked the priest, mildly. 'Something worthy to be followed.'

'It is beautiful,' said James.

'Which part of it, then, offends you?' asked the priest. 'Which part has made you an enemy?'

'Allow that I do not see myself as an enemy,' said James. 'Allow that I am seeking the good.'

'You may think so,' said the priest. She stood. 'But you do not see, as I see.' She was speaking now almost to herself. She examined the intricacies of her tattooed arms. 'You do not know your history.'

She walked to the door and opened it. As she was about to exit, she looked back. 'We have done so much,' she said.

'We?' said James.

'You. I. Humans. Everything you see, James.' She spoke as if in a trance. 'Our arts have blossomed. Our knowledge has swollen. We began—not I, but them, long ago—in the dirt, scratching our way to tools and words and language. Look now, James. Look around you. Look at the glass, the stone, the literature. Look at my arms. Look at *you,* look at your mind! Look at the loveliness!

Think of all who came before us that we might be who we are, and be grateful.'

Her voice fell from her lips, and she became very quiet. In a whisper she continued. 'We stand on the shoulders of giants—but James, you see, this is the difference between you and the Church. *We* seek to become giants ourselves, so that others may someday stand on our shoulders. But *you*—' she shook her head. 'You seek to kill the race of giants.'

She left without another word. High on the wall, the statue of St. Aster cried silent tears.

11

PATIENCE

She left him there for three days.

12

THE TEARS OF ST. ASTER

On the third day the door opened. James was on the floor with his back against the wall. He lifted his hand against the light. He was very cold and very tired.

The lanterns in the ceiling had days ago burned out. When the door closed, the room was once again buried in black. Then—a familiar blue light shone on him, below, and the priest, above.

'This,' said the priest. 'We must speak of it.' She held up James's blue bottle. It was a little more than half full of the same liquid lightning. In its light, her green tattoos looked black as tar.

James watched the bottle sway left and right on the end of its strap. 'It is mine,' he said. 'And it is forbidden.'

'Tell me things I do not already know,' said the priest. 'What is in this bottle?'

'Power,' said James.

'How,' said the priest, slowly, 'did you acquire it?'

'Sorcery. Witchcraft.' James stared at her. 'Human sacrifice. Whatever you like. Through means forbidden to you. The bottle is unclean.'

'I would know what it is,' said the priest.

'It is beyond your power to know,' said James. 'It is—as you say—extra-natural.'

'I will pour it out,' said the priest. And she uncorked the bottle.

'Pour, then,' said James. 'I will fill it again.'

'You will be dead.'

'Then another will fill it.' James lifted his head from the wall. 'It has been discovered. You cannot pour it out of the minds of man. It will be found again and again and it will be used and it will be *good*. Your Church will claim it as your own, two hundred years late, as you did with lemon balm and lavender and St. Aster.'

He leaned his head back and closed his eyes. 'Maybe I'll be St. James, after all. You do love your saints dead.'

The priest relit the lantern and tucked away the blue bottle. 'Very well.'

It seemed to James that the interview was over. But the priest spoke again. 'A passing fancy of the inquiring mind. I will come now to the true meaning of my visit.' She withdrew another bottle, a smaller one, from her robes. Small. Crystal. A vial.

James looked at it with a start. 'My finder's draught.'

'Yes,' said the priest.

'But then—'

'Martha never drank it,' said the priest. 'She intended to, I am sure. Perhaps she felt guilty and could not continue. Perhaps her husband compelled her to confess before she had the chance to use it. Either way, she came to us the night it was delivered to her, all shame and blubber.'

James stood sharply. His breathing was heavy. 'Then the boy has been missing all this time— while you—'

'Hush,' warned the priest. She held up a finger. 'The boy is of age and possesses the free will we are all and one blessed with. His disappearance is not your fault. Nor is it mine.'

'Then he has not been found,' said James.

'We have searched,' said the priest. 'A full party of volunteers and my watchmen, for three days—ever since Martha confessed possession. The strongest force our church had to offer.'

'But he has not been found,' said James.

'No. That is why I am here.' She offered James the vial. 'Drink.'

He stared at it. 'Here? In the very church?'

'It has been decided.' The priest spoke with discomfort. 'The boy may be in danger. The vial can have no further ill effects on your soul than you have already brought on yourself. You may atone, even. Drink. Let good blossom from evil.'

James took the vial. He unstoppered it. He lifted it to his lips, smelled its familiar fragrance, remembered the first time he had successfully *created* such a fluid, how after burns and smokes and red-eyed nights he had finally smelled *this* smell he smelled now. And he paused. He pulled it away.

'No,' he said, and tipped the vial on its side. A drop of clear fluid dangled on the lip.

'What are you doing?' cried the priest.

'Atone!' laughed James. 'I made this. I cannot be both sin and solution.' He tipped it right side up and proffered it to the priest. 'You drink.'

'I!' said the priest. She could not hide her surprise. 'I cannot.'

'You will,' said James.

'I tell you, I cannot,' said the priest.

'Then it goes,' said James, and tipped the vial again.

'Fool!' hissed the priest. 'You would let a child vanish to prove a point?'

'You would let the same child vanish to protect your vanity?' said James. He tipped the vial further. A fat drop spilled its blood on the table.

'You must drink,' said the priest. Her voice had lost its power.

'Yes, I must,' said James, steadily. 'Or else the crowd gathered in front of the church will riot.

They're near to it already. You've promised them a compromise. You've told them you'd descend with the forbidden vial and come up with the heretic who'd sin to find the boy! You look the hero; I stay the villain; but in truth I save you.'

The color had gone out of the priest's face and James knew he had guessed correctly.

'And when instead you come up alone,' James continued, 'they *will* riot. They do not share your convictions. At midday service they do. When it comes down to their lives and their bread and their sons they do not. They will demand the vial be taken, one way or another. What will you tell them? What will you say?'

The priest licked her lips. 'What *will* I say?' she asked, and her question was sincere.

13

HERETICS, ALL

A CROWD WAITED ABOVE. Martha was there, of course, and her husband, and Amity, and a handful of the people who had received illicit materials from James in the weeks he had lived among them, and a group of watchmen. The few beggar children of Promise perched in branches along the street. All waited in breathless quiet. The summer sun fell down in flakes, patching through cloud and leaf in patterns of cat-back and moss.

'That devil of a woman must bring him soon,' muttered Martha.

'Hush, woman,' said her husband. 'D'you want to burn as well?' They were both anxious.

The crowd was anxious too. 'I'll get Victory to brew another! She must know how!' cried a voice. Numerous voices assented.

'Quiet! Heresy!' whispered still more voices.

The doors of the church swung open. 'The priest! The priest!' called the crowd. And the priest it was, smiling faintly, holding a rope. Leashed behind her, bound at the wrists, came James.

'Behold, the heretic!' called the priest, her voice near-ethereal, her eyes a righteous fire. 'He is atoning for his sin; he has taken the poisonous draught himself.' She dragged James to the front of the platform. 'Take us there,' she said.

James wavered on his feet, as if he had only one leg. 'I see—I see—' and he began to walk. The priest walked a step behind him, leash in hand. The crowd followed. The children left the trees and trailed behind.

His steps took them out of Promise, briskly. Past the Parish place on the boundary; into the forest; through thicket and puddle and the tall grass, until at last they reached a clearing within a grove of apple trees.

The trees ringed the clearing in perfect circle, bearing circular fruit. A circular pool, clear and almost sparkling in the light that reached it, graced the center of the clearing. That there was magic in the air was not deniable.

The priest slowed her steps as she entered. 'This place is forbidden.'

'Then the boy may be in real danger,' said James. 'I feel him.'

The priest turned to the crowd. 'Family only.'

Martha and her husband stepped through. The rest fell away a few steps beyond the ring of apple trees, grumbling. But they remained nearby.

'He is here,' said the priest, and her voice was breathless and outside of herself.

'Yes,' said James. 'I feel him.'

Martha's eyes took in the clearing for the first time, took in its obvious emptiness. 'Here! I see nothing. Then—'

'Fear not,' said the priest, and reached out a hand to touch Martha's shoulder. Martha slapped it away. 'No!' she screamed.

'Woman!' hissed her husband.

But Martha would not be contained. 'My son! Dead! Rotting! In a forbidden grove, and not yet sixteen—and for what!' She was spitting now, and the tears fell hot. 'He could have been found days ago—alive!'

'Peace,' said the priest, but she choked on her words, and the voice was still not her own. 'Let the heretic confirm and bring us to your son.'

They turned to James. He had a solemn look on his face. He crossed his arms. 'I will not.'

Martha's tears ran in the silence. 'What? James—please—'

'I am sorry, Martha,' said James. 'But what I mean is, I cannot. I did not drink the finder's draught.'

'Silence!' roared the priest.

'She did,' said James, pointing at the priest.

And those gathered looked.

'A lie,' said the priest. But the magic of the draught was in her voice. A tingle. A waver. How had they missed it?

James noticed that the crowd had begun to spill in through the cracks of the trees.

Martha and her husband stood arm in arm, their faces irreverent. The husband spoke first. 'You drank? You brought us here?'

'A lie,' repeated the priest, eyeing the crowd. 'My lips are pure.'

'Your hands are dirty,' said Martha. 'I'll find him myself.' And she unclasped her hand from her husband's and searched.

The clearing was not large. Martha ran around, here sprinting, here almost on hand and knee, praying imperceptibly, begging that she might find her son sleeping somewhere under a bush. But as she exhausted the periphery, she turned at last to the pool in the center of the clearing. She approached it a-tremble. Before she could look down into it, she turned her sweating face to the priest. She searched for words and found none.

She looked down into the pool.

For a long time Martha did not move. Her husband waited and twitched his fingers. James was a statue. The priest hung her head. Nobody spoke. Nobody breathed. Then—

'He's in here, Tom,' said Martha, with a strange calm. 'Come help me fish him out.'

'Leave it!' said the priest, suddenly. She came to life. 'This grove is forbidden ground. The boy's body must stay here.'

Martha did not turn. Tom kissed her hand and slipped beneath the surface of the water.

'Spirits live here,' urged the priest. The finder's draught was draining from her voice, and she sounded almost herself. The fear was real. 'The extra-natural. The in-human. Please. You must listen.'

'Nobody will listen,' said Martha. Tom emerged, dripping, bearing the corpse. Together they walked, the body on its father's back. They gave James a nod of thanks. They did not look at the priest at all.

14

TIME PASSES AGAIN

T HERE WAS A TRIAL, of course, but it was over quickly. The church would not declare James innocent, but for fear of a riot, they granted him a pardon under 'extenuating circumstances.' They also sent word to the church in Melvale that James was being 'dealt with.'

Under the looming threat of hemorrhaging congregants, the priest announced at midday service that she planned to recommend a revision of doctrine to the church leadership in the City Olivine at their fall convocation. The revision, she said, would seek to explore a more balanced, more nuanced, approach to alchemy. Perhaps, she said, this *was* an art of sorts after all, and James a true artist. All said guardedly, all said to save face —but said, nevertheless.

And in the meantime James was permitted to open a shop in Promise.

Church attendance waned, for some time; then, as new doctrine took hold, it swelled. James attended. Many others who had left returned.

The use of certain mixtures was still forbidden. But the rules were loosened. James took pleasure in teaching the priest herself the proper method of brewing a potion of eloquence—one that, for a time, caused the tongue to burn with fire and panache. The priest's lesson at service that day received a standing ovation.

The church found itself quicker and more skilled in its arts than ever before. Their books flowed out of them as their very blood; their statues almost carved themselves. The time soon came when the trial of James Chalk seemed to the townspeople as ancient history as the burning of St. Aster.

James spent most of his time in his shop, dead in the center of town. He hung a brass sign that read:

Chalk's Apothecary
Fair Dealings — Herbs Bought and Sold

Business was brisk. Money and culture ran through the shop like water. James often taught class after midday service, mixing basic medicines

—and sometimes more exotic brews—with village children interested in the apothic arts. His popularity knew no bounds. From morning till store-close, he was pelted with questions as a peddler of knowledge: 'Is it possible to read the mind of another?' 'Can you teach me to run more quickly?' 'Show me, sir, the path to wealth—' and as he could, James would answer.

But there was one question he would not answer, and, after months of trying, the people learned not to ask.

The question was, of course:

'What is in your little blue bottle?'

15

THE BOY

A BOY PLACED a pile of mint on the counter.

'Just this?' asked James.

'Yes, sir,' said the boy.

'A penny,' said James.

The boy paid. He paced the edges of the room and smelled the stacked herbs. He stopped in a patch of sunlight by the window. He breathed very deep.

At last he waved and left.

James took a leaf that had dropped to the counter and crushed it between his fingers. The smell was pleasant. Mint was pleasant. A weak herb, good for little—but pleasant.

His eyes wandered over the shelves and stock of his shop. Herbs and roots, dried, bound, bottled, lined the walls. Bundles of blossomrod sat proudly on the counter. Better than the shop in

Melvale. James put the mint leaf into his mouth and chewed a moment, two moments—then went to the door, bolted it, and drew the shades.

The shades were thick and blacked the room handily. In the darkness James heard himself breathing. He tried to slow it down. Slowly he did. Some drifting sounds of chatter and trade wafted through his walls, but inside the shop, the herbs and their salesman were silent.

James sat on the floor and spat out the wet mint. He trembled and pulled the little blue bottle from his pocket, then sat it down on the packed earth beneath him. He looked at it for a long time.

The boy came back the next day.

'A penny of mint,' he asked and was granted. He paced, and looked, and left.

He was back the next day, and the next. Each day James's incredulity grew. Mint only, mint alone! Not paired, a part of no brew! With no guisewort or greatleaf to make a sleeping-draught; with no gorse or honeydrop for energy; mint only the boy bought.

On the fifth day James took the boy's hand. 'What do you plan to do with this mint?' he asked, gently.

The boy blinked. 'Sir?'

'The mint, child,' said James. 'A plain herb. Not much you can be doing with it.'

'There's not much I want with it, sir,' said the boy, respectfully. 'Tea, or for chewing, or to dry for the winter.'

'And what,' asked James, 'will you do with it in the winter?'

'Tea,' said the boy. 'Or for chewing.'

James let go of the boy's hand and took a long look at him. He was small. His feet were bare. His elbows stuck out in odd ways.

'Let me make you some tea now,' he said.

James kept a pot of water boiling on the back counter, for potions, mostly, but water was water. He put some of the boy's mint in a stone cup and poured some of the water over it. He poured another cup for himself.

'Here,' he said, and passed the boy the cup. The boy put his hands around it.

James pushed the boy's penny across the counter. 'A refund,' he said. 'The tea is on me.'

The boy took it. 'I thank you.'

They spoke and drank. The boy was an orphan and lived alone off somewhere. He begged on corners and made enough to get by.

At length James cleared his throat. 'You know, child, what I do here?'

The boy nodded.

'You know the powers, then, of mixed medicines? The speed of the birds, the strength of the sun, in your legs and your back?'

'I know of it, sir,' said the boy.

James leaned closer.

'Yet you come here for taste alone, for what a common garden could supply. Wouldn't you like some guisewort? Or honeydrop?' he asked. 'Powerful. A mix of the two, with the mint, of course—'

'I'm not interested in the extra-natural, sir,' the boy said.

'The church has changed,' smiled James. 'Come to my class, tomorrow. I will teach you.'

'I thank you,' said the boy. 'But I am not interested.'

'No?' asked James.

'No,' said the boy.

'Your mint will go farther,' said James. 'Then you needn't come here so often.'

The boy looked around the shop. 'But I enjoy it here, sir.'

'Your life may go farther,' pressed James.

'It goes far enough already, sir,' said the boy, and bowed. And with a wave he was gone.

James watched the door close behind him.

He sighed and rested his hands on the table. Here was a boy who could not be reasoned with.

He examined the little blue bottle. It was half full, a little more, even. Perhaps two-thirds.

Maybe one more.

The next time the boy returned, James put some guisewort in his tea.

16

THE PURCHASE, THE PRICE

IT IS DARK, it is night, it is storming again. James nearly prays but does not. The boy's body fits in his wheelbarrow, and it is this breathing burden James pushes down the road through the puddles and cats. The blue bottle-light, two-thirds full of sloshing brilliance, hangs around his neck. His salted eyes look straight ahead. He does not dare or desire to look down.

He remembers the girl. He remembers how little he felt, the day he discovered the lightning and the price that it would exact on him. He re-members the willingness with which he paid.

He remembers the runaway Daniel. He re-members the grove, and the pool, and the silence with which he paid again.

Against his will he looks down into the wheelbarrow. The boy is an orphan, he reminds himself. A lover of mint and of play and of sleep, but the world is full of these lovers and needs none of them. Where was the boy going? Nowhere. Where was James going? To the river.

He reaches the bridge and goes down to the bank. He throws a handful of herbs into the water and mutters a few words. The water stirs against itself, and from it rises a man, or the form of a man. James bows.

'I have brought it,' he says.

The man in the water waits.

'And this is the last one,' says James, nearly asking, nearly declaring.

The man in the water nearly nods.

'I'll not do another,' says James. 'The third, the last.'

The figure does nothing. James runs a hand through his soaked salt hair. He licks his lips. He looks at the little blue bottle around his neck.

'Very well,' he says, and lifts the wheelbarrow until its tiny burden slides soundlessly into the water. The water-man takes the boy in his arms, spins him gently, kisses his brow, and then he and he both are no more.

James blinks rain from his eyes. He fumbles with the bottle. He unstoppers it and holds it high above his head. He chants. A summons. Lightning strikes, strikes at him directly. The bottle—the bottle!—it catches the bolt and shakes. James's face burns with blue light. For a moment his hands tremble with it, his knees buckle in astonishment, and his eyes widen as the bottle is filled. Filled!

As soon as it starts it is over. The bottle is full. The boy is gone. The lightning's thunder cracks like a whip.

And now for the drinking. And now for the strength. James tips the bottle, up, up! Up to to the star-specked sky! And the lightning slithers down his throat. It tastes of poetry and decades of science—it tastes of pepper and salt and of spices—it is history, and alchemy, and the sum of all knowledge. It runs through him and in him— and he can see it, taste it, touch it.

But as the lightning burns through his brain he realizes—in an instant of horrifying and total enlightenment—he cannot *hold* it. His body is no bottle. The lightning judges him—it finds him wanting—in a moment too short for a gasp or a thought, the body of James Chalk slides into the river. His mouth gives up his breath, and with it the lightning. And the lightning strikes the sky.